PR/

DON
New York
ron._____

DARK KINGS SERIES

DARK WARRIORS SERIES

**Don't miss these other spellbinding novels by
DONNA GRANT**

ROGUES OF SCOTLAND SERIES

The Craving
The Hunger

CHIASSON SERIES

Wild Fever
Wild Dream
Wild Need

DARK KING SERIES

Dark Heat
Darkest Flame
Fire Rising
Burning Desire
Hot Blooded

DARK WARRIOR SERIES

Midnight's Master
Midnight's Lover
Midnight's Seduction
Midnight's Warrior
Midnight's Kiss
Midnight's Captive
Midnight's Temptation
Midnight's Promise
Midnight's Surrender

DARK SWORD SERIES

Dangerous Highlander
Forbidden Highlander

Wicked Highlander
Untamed Highlander
Shadow Highlander
Darkest Highlander

SHIELD SERIES

A Dark Guardian
A Kind of Magic
A Dark Seduction
A Forbidden Temptation
A Warrior's Heart

DRUIDS GLEN SERIES

Highland Mist
Highland Nights
Highland Dawn
Highland Fires
Highland Magic
Dragonfyre

SISTERS OF MAGIC TRILOGY

Shadow Magic
Echoes of Magic
Dangerous Magic

Royal Chronicles Novella Series

Prince of Desire
Prince of Seduction
Prince of Love
Prince of Passion

Wicked Treasures Novella Series

Seized by Passion
Enticed by Ecstasy
Captured by Desire

**And look for more anticipated novels
from Donna Grant**

Moon Kissed (LaRue)
Hot Blooded (Dark Kings)
The Tempted – (Rogues of Scotland)

coming soon!

THE HUNGER

ROGUES OF SCOTLAND

DONNA GRANT

This is a work of fiction. All of the characters, organizations, and events portrayed in this novel are either products of the author's imagination or are used fictitiously.

THE HUNGER

© 2014 by DL Grant, LLC
Excerpt from *Burning Desire* copyright © 2014 by Donna Grant

Cover design © 2014 by Leah Suttle

ISBN 10: 0991454294
ISBN 13: 978-0991454297

Available in ebook and print editions

www.DonnaGrant.com

ACKNOWLEDGEMENTS

A special thanks goes out to my wonderful team that helps me get these books out. Hats off to my editor, Chelle Olsen, and cover design extraordinaire, Leah Suttle. Thank you both for helping me to keep my crazy schedule and keeping me sane!

There's no way I could do any of this without my amazing family – Steve, Gillian, and Connor – thanks for putting up with my hectic schedule and for knowing when it was time that I got out of the house. And special nod to the Grant pets – all five – who have no problem laying on the keyboard to let me know it's time for a break.

Last but not least, my readers. You have my eternal gratitude for the amazing support you show me and my books. Y'all rock my world. Stay tuned at the end of this story for a sneak peek of *Hot Blooded*, Dark Kings book 4 out December 30, 2014. Enjoy!

xoxo
Donna

PROLOGUE

Highlands of Scotland
Summer, 1427

There was something about being with friends. Morcant Banner never thought he would consider three men not related to him brothers, but there was a connection between Stefan, Daman, Ronan, and himself that none could deny. Even more so than the brothers he did have by blood.

Even now as they waited in the valley for Ronan to join them, Morcant basked in the summer sun, contentment settling around him. All his worries vanished when he was with his friends.

Because they accepted him for who he was.

Because no one else would.

The sound of a horse's whinny had all three of them looking to their right and the rider atop the mountain. Ronan. Morcant smiled, anticipation for the evening building.

Ronan leaned forward slightly. His horse pawed at the ground and then raced down the mountain at breakneck speed. Stefan shook his head at Ronan's recklessness, while Morcant and Daman laughed.

Morcant held his stallion with a firm hand as the horse yearned to race as well. Morcant got him under control just as Ronan arrived.

"About time," Stefan grumbled crossly.

Ronan raised his brow. "You might want to rein in that temper, my friend. We're going to be around beautiful women this night. Women require smiles and sweet words. No' furrowed brows."

There was laughter from everyone but Stefan, who gave Ronan a humorless look.

"Aye, we've heard enough about this Ana," Daman said as he turned his mount alongside Ronan's. "Take me to this gypsy beauty so I can see her for myself."

Ronan's lips compressed. "You think to take her from me?"

Daman's confident smile grew as his eyes twinkled in merriment. "Is she that beautiful?"

"Just you try," Ronan dared, only half jesting.

"Be cautious, Ronan. You wrong a gypsy, and they'll curse you. No' sure we should be meddling with such people," Morcant said as he shoved his hair out of his eyes. He knew the stories of the gypsies, and it gave him just enough caution and prudence that might not otherwise be there.

Then again, the young gypsy women were known for their beauty and seductive ways.

Morcant couldn't say no to that. Hell, what sane man could?

Ronan laughed and reined in his jittery mount. "Ah, but with such a willing body, how am I to refuse Ana? Come, my friends, and let us enjoy the bounty that awaits." He gave a short whistle and his horse surged forward in a run.

Morcant and the others remained behind for a moment as they watched Ronan take the lead as he always did. It had begun a decade earlier when they chanced upon each other during Highland Games between their four clans. After that, they made sure to meet up regularly until they were as inseparable as brothers. The four formed a friendship that grew tighter with each year that passed.

"I'm no' missing this," Morcant said and gave his stallion his head.

The horse immediately took off. Behind him, Morcant could hear the thundering of Stefan's and Daman's horse's hooves.

Ronan looked over his shoulder, a wide smile on his face. He spurred his mount faster. Not to be outdone, Morcant leaned low over his stallion's neck until he pulled up alongside Ronan.

One by one, the three caught up with Ronan. A few moments later, Ronan tugged the reins, easing his stallion into a canter until they rode their horses four abreast. A glance showed that even Stefan's face had eased into lines that some could consider almost a smile.

The four rode from one glen to another until Ronan finally slowed his horse to a walk. They stopped atop the next hill and looked down at the circle of gypsy wagons hidden in the wooded vale below.

Need pounded through Morcant. It was always the same. Women. He loved women. They were meant to be sheltered and protected, and made love to for hours until they were boneless and sated.

He made it his life's mission to woo and pleasure as many women as he could. His mother said it seemed as if his soul searched for something – or someone.

In fact, it was the opposite. Morcant wasn't looking for anyone that would tie him down. His duties to his clan were all he would ever need or want.

"I've a bad feeling," Daman said as he shifted uncomfortably atop his mount. "We shouldna be here."

Morcant's horse flung up his head, and he brought his mount under control with soft words. "I've a need to sink my rod betwixt willing thighs. If you doona wish to partake, Daman, then doona, but you willna be stopping me."

"Nor me," Ronan said.

Stefan was silent for several moments before he gave Ronan a nod of agreement.

Ronan was the first to ride down the hill to the camp, and Morcant was right on his heels. He watched in interest as a young beauty with long, black hair came running out to greet Ronan in her brightly colored skirts. Ronan pulled his horse to a halt and jumped off with a smile as Ana launched herself into his arms. Ronan caught her and brought his lips down to hers. It was a reunion of lovers, and Morcant began to scan the female faces for his own. After all, why spend the night alone when there were willing women around?

Ronan and Ana spoke quietly before Ronan turned her toward them. "Ana, these are my friends, Daman, Morcant, and Stefan," he said, pointing to each of them in turn.

Her smile was wide as she held out her arm to the camp. "Welcome to our camp."

Morcant didn't wait on the others to dismount. He'd already found what he was looking for. He dropped the reins to allow his horse to graze freely and walked between two wagons into the center of the camp.

He glanced behind him to find Stefan following. Morcant paused when he noticed the indecision on Daman's face. It was long moments until Daman slid from his horse and gathered the reins of all four mounts to tether them together.

"I'll keep watch," Daman said as he sat outside the camp near a tree.

Ronan wrapped an arm around Ana and walked away, his voice calling, "Your loss."

Morcant gave a nod to Daman and then continued on his way to the woman he'd seen sitting on the steps to her wagon, her bright turquoise and yellow skirts dipping between her legs while she braided a leather halter for a horse.

"Och, but you're a bonny lass," Morcant said as

he leaned against the side of the wagon.

Her dark eyes cut to look at him suspiciously. "I'm alone for a reason."

"And that is?"

"Not your concern," she said and went back to her braiding.

Morcant moved so that he stood in front of her. It took several moments before she lifted her black gaze to his. Her dark hair was down, the thick waves falling over her shoulders, begging to be touched.

"A woman should be protected. Why do you no' have someone protecting you?"

She shrugged and glanced around her. "I am protected. Look around. These people, my people, are my protection."

"But you're lonely."

It wasn't a question, and when she paused in her plaiting for a second time, Morcant stepped closer. "Why are you alone?" he pressed.

"My grandmother foretold that I would meet my husband on my travels, and that I must remain pure for him. That husband would give me a baby that would unite the gypsy clans in Romania. If I were to remain pure."

Morcant couldn't believe her words. Even if the foretelling were true, which he highly doubted, the gypsy was beautiful with her olive skin and large eyes. "It's difficult to refuse the pleasures of the flesh," he said as he guessed what had happened by the regret in her gaze.

"More than I ever imagined."

"Such a waste to leave someone so lovely on her own. Your family should be with you."

"I was part of a great prophecy that I ruined. My family shunned me," she said in a whisper, her eyes locking with his.

"I'm Morcant."

Her lips softened into another smile. "Denisa."

He closed the small gap between them. "I offer nothing more than pleasure."

"I shouldn't," she said softly.

Morcant touched her face with his fingers before he rubbed his thumb along her lower lip. "There's nothing wrong with giving in to your desires. You are sensual and beautiful. You were made to experience pleasure."

Without a word, she set aside the leather strips and stood before ducking into her wagon. Morcant smiled when her hand slid between the curtains and held one side open for him.

~ ~ ~

Morcant had had his share of virgins. It wasn't as if he sought them out. More often than not, they sought him because of his experience and renown for the pleasure he could give. He was well known for his skills as a lover, and he made sure never to leave a woman unsatisfied.

But the gypsy had lied to him. She hadn't given in to another man. He had been her first, which couldn't be good any way he tried to look at it. Why had she lied? He couldn't piece it together, but it didn't matter. He wouldn't be around long enough to learn the truth.

Denisa lay sleeping on her side, her long, black hair tangled and damp with sweat from their exertions. He had pleasured her until she was limp but just as always, nothing stirred within him.

He found his own release, but there was a weight, a deadness that filled him with each woman he slept with. Sometimes he felt as if it might swallow him whole.

Morcant leaned up on his elbow and lightly kissed Denisa on her forehead. He rose and dressed quietly. Now that his needs were seen to, he would sit with Daman until the others finished.

The night was shattered with an anguished scream, a soul-deep, fathomless cry that was wrung from the depths of someone's soul.

"What the hell," Morcant said as he hurried to exit the wagon still fastening his kilt.

His gaze snagged on Daman, who stood standing outside the wagons staring at something with a resigned expression on his face. Morcant turned to see what had caught Daman's attention, and found Ronan, shirtless with his hand on the hilt of his sword as he stood looking at an old woman who gazed down at something in the grass.

That's when Morcant spotted the bright pink and blue skirts of Ana, Ronan's lover. Even in the fading light of evening, there was no mistaking the dark stain upon the grass as anything but blood. Unease rippled through Morcant when he saw the dagger sticking out of Ana's stomach with her hand still around it. The night of pleasure and laughter vanished.

They needed to leave. Morcant shifted his gaze to Stefan, who stood amid a group of gypsies. Stefan gave him a nod.

Morcant began to softly, slowly pull his sword from his scabbard. The gypsies would blame Ana's suicide on Ronan. The only way they would get out of this alive was by killing them all.

"Ronan," Stefan said urgently.

Morcant waited for Ronan to attack, but before Ronan could, the old woman let loose a shriek and pointed her gnarled finger at him. Ronan's eyes widened in confusion and anger.

Morcant heard a rustle behind him as Denisa poked her head out of the wagon. He glanced at her to see sadness fill her eyes. "What is going on?" he demanded in a quiet voice.

"Ana was Ilinca's granddaughter. She's using her magic to keep Ronan in place as she levels her curse upon him."

"Curse?" Morcant felt as if he'd been kicked by a horse. Daman had been right. They should have listened to his warning and never entered the camp.

It would be a miracle if they made it out alive.

Words tumbled from Ilinca's mouth, her wrinkled face a mask of grief and fury. Morcant didn't need to comprehend the words to realize Denisa was right, that Ilinca was cursing Ronan.

Morcant wasn't going to stand still and wait. With his sword in hand, he rushed to Ilinca, ready to take her head. He was a mere four steps away when she turned her furious gaze on him, and froze him in his tracks.

Morcant couldn't move no matter how much he tried. He couldn't shout a warning to Stefan, couldn't demand that Daman get away.

All he could do was watch helplessly as Ilinca went back to cursing Ronan.

The ever-present rage exploded in Stefan and he let out a battle cry worthy of his clan as he leapt over the fire toward Ilinca. But once more, the old gypsy used her magic to halt him.

Her gaze shifted to Daman. Morcant prayed Daman would get help, but they had never left each other behind before. It wouldn't start now. Daman glanced at the ground and inhaled deeply. Then, with purposeful strides, he crossed some unseen barrier into the camp.

Morcant watched as Ronan squeezed his eyes shut, his body fairly vibrating with pain. And then he was gone, vanished as if he had never existed.

Ilinca faced Morcant next. She looked to Denisa's wagon, and her anger grew, becoming palpable. More incomprehensible words fell from her lips.

Morcant didn't have time to think of anything as his sword flew from his hand and pain exploded in his head. He squeezed his eyes shut, but there was no blocking it out. It went on for eternity.

When it finally died, Morcant discovered he could move. But when he opened his eyes, there was nothing but darkness.

And silence.

"This is for ruining Denisa and the foretelling that would unite all gypsies. For that, I curse you, Morcant Banner. Forever will you be locked in this place alone until you earn your freedom."

Morcant didn't feel anything. No heat, no cold, no wind, no rain, no hunger, no thirst. There was no light, no sound, no stirring of anything. He was utterly alone.

Not once had he ever been afraid, but he was now. He sank down and dropped his head in his hands. He hadn't been able to help Ronan, and he didn't know what had happened to Stefan and Daman. How was he to help any of them now when he didn't know where he was or how to get out?

Morcant squeezed his eyes closed and began to hum. Anything to break up the silence.

CHAPTER ONE

1609 Scotland

Leana lifted her face to the wind and closed her eyes. There was a touch of fall upon the air, a nip of icy chill that hinted at the winter to come. She loved autumn, but winter was her favorite season. There was something peaceful and beautiful about the country blanketed in white.

The wind died away, and Leana opened her eyes to see the mountain's gentle slope to the valley below. The small village was all she knew. The people were good and kind. They were simple folk who lived simple lives.

They also meant well, but sometimes they didn't know when to leave well enough alone.

A gust of wind whipped her skirts about her legs violently. Leana adjusted the basket in her hands and turned around to finish her hike up the mountain to the other side where she could find the herbs she searched for.

Leana had walked the hills and mountains alone for as long as she could remember. The fact that the village was in the middle of Clan Sinclair meant that they were rarely raided by other clans. Not to say that the younger men of the village didn't join in with others and raid their closest neighbor – the MacKays.

As soon as she entered the forest, Leana let out a sigh. The forest always relaxed her. It was why she chose to remain in her cottage alone instead of moving to the village. She didn't understand the girls her age who were focused solely on finding a husband. There was more to life than a man.

Leana was alone, but she wasn't lonely. People tended to get the two confused, or assumed that she must be lonely because she was alone. Truth be told, people irritated her. They presumed, interfered, or simply tried to tell her what to do. As if any of it would work. Yet, no matter how many years passed, they continued on as they were, claiming it was for her own good.

As if they knew her well enough to know what was good for her.

Leana stopped and set her basket down as she knelt next to a bog myrtle shrub. She broke off several stems. The plant was used for a variety of applications, such as including it in her bedding to ward off insects, and occasionally adding it to her candles to help put her to sleep, especially when she combined some lavender into the wax, as well.

When she finished, Leana rose and continued her stroll through the ferns and trees. She found a small meadowsweet bush. Not only was it a great herb to cure headaches or calm nerves, but the leaves could also be used to treat sores. Leana took only a little of the meadowsweet so there would be more later.

She replenished more of her stock of herbs on her walk. Leana strolled leisurely through the trees, touching them as she passed. There were some so huge, her arms couldn't wrap half way around them. There were others so tall she was sure the tops brushed the clouds.

Songbirds chirped happily, filling the air with a continuous melody that seemed to grow louder and louder. Leana saw a wildcat out of the corner of her eye, but she knew better than to try and coax the animal to her. It would stay hidden until she left.

After another half hour of walking and collecting herbs, Leana sat against a tree and leaned her head back. Her eyes drifted shut and her mind began to drift as it often did when she was in the forest.

Except it wasn't the brush of a breeze on her cheek she felt. It was…emptiness. This was no dream. She calmed her racing heart when she realized she was having a vision. At first, there was nothing but darkness all around her sucking all the light. She couldn't see her hand in front of her face. Slowly, gradually she began to make out the shape of a man. He was down on one knee, hunched over so that his left hand was braced on the ground. He fisted his right hand and then spread his fingers, only to repeat the movements again and again. His sandy blonde hair hung loose and wavy around him, hiding his face from view.

He wore a saffron shirt and kilt, along with black boots. There was nothing that could hide the hard sinew that bunched in his arms and shoulders, or the fury that radiated from him as intensely as the rays of the sun.

Suddenly, he stilled. Then his head slowly turned to her, and he pinned her with his yellow-brown gaze that flared as bright as a topaz.

~ ~ ~

Morcant stood. He sat. He crawled, he kneeled, he even lay prone, but nothing helped. He shouted, he whispered. He cursed.

And he prayed.

His hand missed the feel of his sword. He missed the weight of the weapon, the leather-wrapped pommel, and the way the blade sounded when he swung it. The sword was his pride and joy, it was the only thing that meant anything to him other than the men he considered brothers – Stefan, Ronan, and Daman.

Where were they? Had the gypsy killed them? Perhaps she threw them in a prison like him. Saints, he hoped that wasn't the case. He didn't know how long he had been in the darkness, but he knew it was a considerable amount of time. Or perhaps it had only been a blink in time.

The fact he didn't need to eat or sleep worried him at first. That was soon forgotten as he realized the one thing that he couldn't relieve or ignore was his cock. He was in a constant state of arousal, and if he touched himself, it only made the need double.

Was this his punishment for sleeping with the lovely Denisa? She'd said she wasn't a virgin, but Morcant knew he would've likely taken her even if she had been honest. He had wanted a woman, and she was beautiful and willing.

He fell to his knee and closed his eyes as he concentrated on remembering what it felt like to hold his sword. He fisted his hand, just to spread his fingers wide and fist his hand again and again and again.

His balls tightened, and his cock jumped as a swell of desire shot through him. In his mind, he recalled how it felt to sink into the warm, wet flesh of a woman's sex, to have her legs wrap around him.

Sweat broke out over him as he fought not to grab his cock and attempt to ease the devastating, engulfing hunger of his body. He fell to one knee and braced himself with his left hand, his fingers splayed upon the ground.

Not once in all his years before had he denied himself sex. The act allowed him pleasure, as well as the chance to lose himself for a few moments before he realized just how devoid his life truly was.

Morcant didn't know how long he remained in that position until he was able to think past the need clawing through him. When he could take a deep breath, he had the sensation that he was being watched.

He opened his eyes and slowly turned his head, but he saw nothing. Nothing but black as far as he could see. What he wouldn't do to see some color, even if it were the gray skies that could last for weeks in his beloved Scotland.

As dark as it was, Morcant could see himself when he looked down, but if there were anything or anyone else in the cursed place, he couldn't see or hear them.

He clenched his teeth. Morcant tried to remember Denisa's face and body, tried to recall how it had felt when he had lain with her, but he couldn't remember anything about her. There had even been a few occasions where he forgot her name.

When that happened, he would go through everyone he knew and recount their names as well as what they looked like because his fear was that he would lose himself in the blackness.

Perhaps he already had. His friends might be trying to wake him up, and he didn't even know it.

Or he could be dead and this was Hell.

He wouldn't claim to be a saint, but neither had he done enough to have his soul condemned to Hell. It could be purgatory, or it could be nothing. How many times had Morcant gone over this in his head? How many times had he talked out loud, hoping that something might make more sense if he heard it?

He was losing his mind. Bit by bit, little by little, the longer he remained in this wretched place, the more of him was taken.

He fought against it, but it did no good. The gypsy had seen to that.

CHAPTER TWO

Leana's eyes snapped open, her heart pounding against her ribs. She wasn't sure what she had witnessed.

Everything had been too real. The darkness, the stillness. Then there was the man himself. She heard his ragged breathing, sensed the battle he waged within himself. She felt the warmth of his skin and was pierced by his topaz eyes.

As her breathing calmed, Leana recalled the man's face. She only had a glimpse, but his image was embedded in her mind. Sharp eyes, slender nose, hard jaw, sunken cheeks that accentuated his cheekbones, and too-wide lips. Whether she wanted to remember him or not, she didn't have a choice.

Leana shook her head to clear it. It had to have been a dream. There was no such man about the area, nor such a place of blackness. She always dreamed in the woods, though they weren't really dreams. She sometimes saw the future. It was just glimpses, barely blips of images that came to her, but days, weeks, or even months later, what she dreamt would come to pass.

Excitement blossomed in her chest at the thought that she might get to see the man. That emotion died a swift death as she recalled his anger. No, it would be better if she forgot the dream and the man.

Leana got to her feet and dusted herself off before reaching for her basket. She began to walk back to the cottage, and that's when she realized how noisy the forest was. Halting, she looked up to the branches and saw birds everywhere.

All around her birds perched, looking down at her as they sang loudly. In all the times Leana had been in the forest, she had never seen so many birds or heard them singing so deafeningly. She lifted her skirts in her free hand and lengthened her strides. The day was an unusual one, and she wanted it behind her.

Leana hadn't gotten far when she slipped on the dead leaves. Her basket flew from her hands as she struggled to keep her footing and not tumble down the steep slope of the mountain.

She cried out as her feet came out from beneath her and she fell on her rump, sliding as she did. Leana grasped a passing tree and managed to stop herself. She pulled herself into a sitting position. The birds were fluttering now, their songs getting louder.

Leana covered her ears and looked down the mountain to her basket that had crashed against a giant oak, her herbs scattered. She stood on shaky legs and slowly made her way to the basket. It wasn't until she began to gather the herbs that the birds started to swoop around her. Leana hurriedly tossed the herbs into her basket, looking up as she did.

Her hand closed around something cold and metal. As soon as it did, the birds stopped singing. A moment later, their wings halted as they returned to the branches. The stillness was unnerving, but it was nothing compared to the utter silence.

Leana turned her head and looked down to see what it was she had grabbed. She frowned and pulled it out from beneath the ferns to reveal a sword. She marveled at the size of it. Even with both her hands on the pommel, there was still room. It was made for a man with large hands, a man with strength enough to wield such a weapon.

Slowly, she withdrew the weapon from the scabbard to look upon the blade itself. It was flawless. She tested one edge by running the pad of her thumb across the blade and saw a small line of blood bubble from her skin.

Why would anyone leave such a weapon behind? Leana fit the sword back into the scabbard. Whatever the reason, the weapon was now hers. She would learn to use it just as she had her brother's bow and arrows. It wasn't going to be easy, but she was more than capable of taking care of herself. And she would prove it once again.

Leana carried the sword in one hand and the basket in the other. She rose and turned around, only to freeze. Not five feet from her lay an unconscious man with long, sandy blonde hair in the same tartan she had seen in her vision. The sword fell from her numb fingers. She could only stare in shock. It was as if her vision had brought him to life.

She set the basket down carefully and hesitantly walked to him. Leana knelt beside him. Several seconds passed before she reached out and warily moved a portion of his hair that covered half his face.

As soon as she did, there was a flutter of wings as the birds suddenly took to the skies and flew away. She watched them for a moment before she turned her attention back to the man.

Leana was enraptured by the striking male. His skin was deeply tanned, and there was a short beard of a darker blonde than his hair covering his face that did nothing to hide the hard lines of his jaw and chin.

She let her fingers brush over the beard, amazed at how soft the bristles were. That's when her gaze snagged on a scar that ran along his face from his right temple into his hairline. It was jagged and looked as though it went deep. How she wanted to know what caused such a scar.

Her gaze leisurely drank in his amazing face from his brows that matched his beard, to his crooked nose, to his mouth. Her eyes then drifted lower to the open expanse of his saffron shirt that revealed lean muscle honed to perfection.

Leana swallowed hard and, unable to help herself, pulled open his shirt a little more. She told herself it was to look for a wound, but she knew it was to see more of such a fine specimen. He was unlike any man she had ever encountered – or was likely to see again.

His skin was warm, as if the sun had been upon him. Something that was difficult in the deep shade of the tall trees. She bit her lip as she flattened her hand upon his chest. Beneath her palm, she could feel the steady beat of his heart. His breathing was even, but that didn't explain why he was unconscious.

Leana began to worry that there really was a wound she couldn't see. She forgot her exploration of his fine body and began to smooth her hands gently over his torso. She touched his side, only to have his fingers clamp around her wrist. Her eyes jerked to his face to find him staring at her. She opened her mouth to speak but didn't get a sound out as she was suddenly on her back with him leaning over her.

"Who are you?" His voice was deep, raspy, as if it hadn't been used in awhile.

She was taken aback by the intensity of his golden brown eyes. "Leana."

"Is this a trick?" he asked with a frown.

Leana shook her head, all too aware of his very male body atop her. She liked the feel of him entirely too much. His muscles. His weight. His…hardness that pressed into her stomach.

"Nay."

His topaz eyes lifted from hers to glance quickly around. "How am I here?"

"I don't know. One moment you weren't, and the next you were. I was attempting to see if you had an injury." She twisted her wrists that he held in each hand to remind him he had a hold of her.

His frown faded when he looked at her wrists, and then he slowly returned his gaze to her. Gone was the confusion, replaced by blatant desire. Leana's blood heated instantly, and her nipples tightened at the look in his eyes. If he could make her feel like that with just a look, what would happen if he touched her?

Morcant fought against the desire, rallied against the vast hunger to sate himself on such a woman until neither could move. He remained still and prayed the lass did the same. If she moved, he wasn't sure he would be able to keep himself in check. As if sensing how perilously close he was to losing control, she grew so still she was barely breathing.

He couldn't believe he was out of the darkness. His mind was a jumble of questions, as his senses were bombarded with sounds and sights. He wanted to soak it all in, but he couldn't make himself move off the woman.

She was a bonny lass with rich, brown hair and eyes as blue as the sky. Those eyes watched him carefully, her fear kept hidden. She stared at him, unblinking, as if she were trying to decide if he were real.

Her heart-shaped face was beyond lovely. There was something in the curve of her full lips and the direct stare of her sky blue eyes that was both accepting and curious. He longed to stroke his fingers down her smooth cheek to her neck, and lower to her breasts pressed against him.

Her soft curves that cradled his body were only clouding his mind. His cock ached to be inside her, to relieve the torment that had been his for countless days.

"You were in the darkness," she said in a soft whisper.

His brow furrowed as he recalled sensing someone watching him not long before he was suddenly jerked out of his prison so hard that he blacked out. "How do you know that?"

"I...I saw it."

"Impossible."

She lifted a brow. "As impossible as you suddenly appearing? Were you in darkness?"

He debated whether to answer her. Who in their right mind would believe a word he said about such a place? Then again, if she *had* seen him, she might be the only one who would believe him. "Aye."

"That place was awful," she said with a shudder.

His desire faded as he thought of his prison and his friends. Morcant rolled off her to sit with his arms resting on his knees. "How did you see me?"

"I don't know," Leana said as she sat up and picked leaves from her long braid. "I sometimes see things that eventually come to pass."

"You see things?" he asked curiously as he turned his head to look at her.

She shrugged and looked down at her faded blue gown. "I don't tell people that normally."

"Who am I to tell?"

There was a hint of a smile as she cut her eyes to him. "True. Where were you, when I saw you?"

"What did you see?" He wanted to know how long she had watched him.

"Not much. I saw you kneeling. I could sense your anger and frustration."

He looked back to the trees. "My ever-present companions."

"Why didn't you leave such a place?"

"I tried. Many times. It was my prison, I suppose you could call it."

Leana's head turned to him. "Prison? Who put you there?"

"A gypsy." Morcant looked at her to see her eyes widen.

"I've heard rumors of the power of gypsy curses. You must have angered her greatly."

Morcant grunted as he recalled that awful night, though Ilinca's fury was mostly directed at Ronan. He knew Stefan and Daman well enough to know both of them would search for him and Ronan until their deaths.

He knew by Leana's brogue that he was still in the Highlands, but he didn't know how far he was from his clan. The sooner he started toward home, the sooner he could meet up with Stefan and

Daman and help them find Ronan, because if he could get out of his prison, then so could Ronan, wherever he was.

"Where am I?"

"The Sinclair clan."

Morcant briefly closed his eyes. He was days away from home. Then another question occurred to him: just how long had he been in his prison. "What year is it?"

"1609. I gather by the muscle jumping in your temple that my answer wasn't what you wanted?"

He laughed, though there was no mirth in the sound. "I knew I was confined for a long time, but I didna think it would be nearly two hundred years."

"Two hundred?" Leana asked with wide eyes. "That can't be correct."

Morcant rose to his feet and walked to a spot of sunlight that filtered through the trees. "The last time I saw the sky, it was the Year of our Lord 1427." He turned his head to her. "I was with three of my closest friends. All I could think about while in the darkness was finding them. Now I know that's impossible, at least for two of them."

"Why?" she asked and climbed to her feet.

"The gypsy that cursed me, Ilinca, was furious over her granddaughter's suicide. She blamed my friend, Ronan. I was trying to help him when she threw me into the darkness. If she didna kill Ronan, he could be in a similar prison."

"And the other two friends?"

Morcant fisted his hands as he itched for his

sword. "They'll either have been smart and gotten away, in which case they're long dead, or..." he trailed off as he considered what could have happened.

"Or," Leana pressed.

"Or they were imprisoned like me."

Leana smoothed out her skirts and eyed him. "If I didn't have glimpses of things to come, or if I hadn't seen you before you appeared, I'd think you were daft. If I were you, I wouldn't repeat any of this to others. Good luck finding your friends."

He nodded his thanks and watched as she bent to pick up a basket. It wasn't until she grasped something else that he realized it was a sword – *his* sword!

Morcant wasn't going anywhere without his sword.

CHAPTER THREE

Leana hadn't gotten three steps before she heard the man following her. He set her on edge, reminded her, as no one else could, that she was alone, likely never to know the touch of a man.

"Hold up, Leana," he said as he hurried to catch up.

She didn't slow her steps. Every time she looked at him, she wanted to wrap her arms around him and beg him to lie atop her once more so she could feel his weight again. It should be wrong for a man's body to feel so good atop her.

"I think you freed me," he said.

She glanced at him. "Perhaps. Make use of it and find your friends."

"I should repay you."

"There's no need," she said as she strode up the hill at a brisk pace.

He stopped and said, "To be honest, I was wondering if I could beg a meal. I have no coin or belongings with which to trade. I doona even have a weapon."

Leana's steps slowed and then halted. She tightened her grip on the sword. Giving it to him wasn't an option, but she could feed him. She turned to face him. "I don't even know your name."

"Morcant Banner, lass," he said with a bright smile.

She knew with such a sexy, rakish smile like his that there were few women who had refused him anything. "Well, Morcant, you have a grand adventure ahead of you. I can't in good conscience send you on your way without a meal."

"That's verra kind of you," he said and closed the distance between them. He reached for the sword, "Let me help you carry that."

Leana easily dodged his hands. "I'm capable of carrying it myself."

He held up his hands and flashed that charming grin. "Forgive me. I just wanted to help."

She continued walking, and he kept pace with her. Leana let the silence go on for a while. He smiled and acted as if everything was fine, but he couldn't hide the pain and confusion in his beautiful topaz eyes.

Leana covertly watched him out of the corner of her eye. He kept fisting his hands, just as she saw him do while in the darkness. The weight of the sword in her hand made her wonder if it was simply a coincidence that she'd found the weapon right before he had appeared – or if the sword were his. There was no doubt he was a man accustomed to having a weapon.

She wasn't as taken aback by his story as others would be because she had encounters with the gypsies before. She had seen, firsthand, what some of them were capable of when they were wronged.

Magic wasn't a word she bandied about, and yet, it was a word she knew all too well, and not just from her experience with the gypsies. Nor did it have anything to do with her visions.

No, the villagers spoke the word often in regards to her. They said her use of herbs to heal was unexplainable, magical. Perhaps it was magic that helped her know which herbs to use for what. She didn't know or care.

Morcant was an oddity, much like herself. Is that why she felt the need to help him? Or was it because she found him all too appealing?

"Did you eat while in the darkness?" she asked to fill the silence.

"Nay. I wasna hungry or thirsty, though I find I'm famished now."

She glanced over to find him looking at her, his eyes watching her curiously. "Do I have leaves in my hair?"

"Nay," he replied softly, a half smile upon his lips. "I just didna expect to finally get out of my prison and be confronted with such a lovely vision."

Leana held back her snort. She didn't take his

words to heart, because she knew while she might look good to a starving man now, he wouldn't remember her afterward.

"You doona believe me?" he said, his voice filled with surprise.

Leana reached the top of the steep incline and shrugged. "You said you didn't feel hunger until you were released. I suppose you didn't feel a man's need until now either."

"You'd be wrong, lass."

His words were laced with fury, causing her gaze to jerk to him. Leana saw the truth shining in his eyes. He hadn't suffered just the darkness. He'd endured unending longing, as well.

She swallowed and quickly looked away when his gaze dropped to her breasts. Leana recalled all too well how delightful he'd felt atop her. "In the valley is a small village. On the edge of town is a widow who lost her much older husband during the winter. She'll be more than willing to take you to her bed."

"You think you know me well enough to know what I want?"

She tried to ignore the scorn in his voice. "I know men."

"I've known a lot of women, but I doona claim to know you because of it."

Leana pushed the stray hairs out of her face from the wind. "It isn't difficult to know a man. You're ruled by your cock, your stomach, and bloodshed."

"Is that so," he replied with a cool look. "Tell

me then, what type of man am I?"

Every instinct screamed for her to walk away and forget his challenge, but when had Leana ever walked away from anything? It was a trait that got her in trouble more times than she could remember. Instead, she faced Morcant and locked gazes with him.

"You're the type of man who easily charms. You're the type of man who is used to getting whatever he wants. You're the type of man who leaves a string of broken hearts wherever he goes. You're the type of man who gives his word to another man, but never to a woman."

For long moments, he simply stared at her. Then he said, "I doona deny loving women. They are meant to be protected and sheltered. They were made to be loved by men, to be brought unimaginable pleasure. If it's wrong that I've given women ecstasy, then condemn me."

"You've already been condemned by the gypsy," Leana pointed out.

"Aye. You've the right of it. I no' only went with my friends, but I did find a willing bed partner before that."

"If she was willing, then why did the gypsy curse you?"

He raked a hand through his long blonde hair and blew out a deep breath as his gaze shifted to the valley and the village. "The woman I bedded told me she'd already had another man before me. She lied."

"She was an innocent?" Leana asked in shock.

Morcant stiffly nodded his head. "I've had women say they were virgins when they were no', but I've never had one claim to be experienced and no' be."

Leana swung her gaze to the village. "Did you confront her with it?"

"What good would it have done?"

"None, I suppose." She turned to the right and began walking.

Morcant's heavy footfalls fell in behind her. "You doona live in the village?"

"Nay."

"What will you tell your husband about me?"

Leana glanced over her shoulder. "Nothing. I don't have a husband."

"Your father, then?"

"He's dead, as are my brothers, my sister, my mother, and my two uncles."

She was a bit surprised when Morcant didn't ask why she lived alone, but she was glad she didn't have to explain it. The rest of the walk to the cottage was done in silence, making her aware of his every move, his every breath until she was anxious to put some distance between them.

Leana jerked to a stop when Morcant's hand suddenly snaked out and grasped her upper arm, drawing her to a stop. Her head snapped to him, realizing too late that she didn't know how to use the sword to defend herself. The one weapon she could use, was inside the cottage.

"How long have you been gone, lass?" he whispered as his gaze surveyed their surroundings.

"I left after the noon meal."

He gave a quick look to the sky. "It's been hours. It's no' wise to walk blithely in there without first ensuring there are no' enemies about."

"The only enemies we have this far onto Sinclair land are the few raiders from the MacKays."

Morcant pointed to the ground a few feet in front of them. "That boot print is much larger than yours. Far afield or no', you can no' be too careful."

A shiver raced through Leana. There was no denying the proof of Morcant's words. "There's been talk over the past few months, but I didn't believe any of it. Old men talk of the past and how things were."

"What are they saying?"

She pulled her eyes away from the ground and the boot print to Morcant. "The MacKays lost many of their warriors in last fall's battle with the Frasers. The Frasers then raided the MacKays and took all their sheep. The MacKay laird was killed trying to get the sheep back, and the clan has been in an uproar ever since. Many have left the clan, and the ones who remained took to raiding during the winter to keep from starving."

"In other words, the men who remain are more bandits and criminals than clansmen," Morcant said with a frown.

Leana swiveled her head from one side to the other looking through the dense trees set behind the cottage to the stream that ran on the left side. "A new laird stepped forward, and he's working to unite his clan once more, but it's been a slow process."

"It doesna bode well for your clan if the raiders are making it this far in without being seen." Morcant made her face him. "Remain here while I have a look inside."

Leana didn't have to be told twice. She was rooted to the spot, watching as Morcant walked cautiously toward the door. She was struck anew with his masculinity and strength.

He bent and picked up a log of wood stacked by the door, the muscles in his forearm flexing as his fingers wrapped around the firewood. The way he stalked the cottage, the way he saw and heard every sound, reminded her of a predator closing in on his prey.

Her breath locked in her lungs when he slowly opened the door and slipped inside. Leana kept waiting to hear a crash as he came upon an intruder, but a moment later he walked back outside.

Morcant put a hand to his lips to keep her quiet when she started to speak. Leana's eyes followed him as he walked around the cottage with the same alert and vigilant motions as before. When she lost sight of him, Leana's gaze jerked to the other side of the cottage and waited for him to reappear. When he did, he walked casually, replacing the log as he did.

"Whoever was here is gone now," he said. "It isna a safe place for you to be alone."

She walked past him through the door into the

cottage. "It's my home. I'm not leaving it."

"You say that as though I'm no' the first to mention it to you."

"Because you're not." Leana set down her herbs on the table before standing the sword next to her bow and quiver of arrows alongside the hearth. "I'll have some food ready shortly."

She heard the chair scrape the boards as he pulled it out and sat. Leana tried to ignore Morcant, but his very presence sucked all the space from the tiny structure.

"What happened to your parents?" he asked.

Leana paused in chopping the carrots. "No one can escape death when it comes for you, and it comes in various ways. My mum died years ago during childbirth. My youngest brother, who was stillborn, is buried with her."

"You mentioned other brothers."

"I had four older brothers and one younger. All sought glory and readily answered the call to go raiding or into battle. Each time one left, they didn't return," she said as she reached for another carrot.

A large hand covered hers, stilling her hand before she could move. Morcant was close behind her, his heat seeping through her clothes. When had he moved? She hadn't heard him, hadn't sensed he'd left the chair.

"That couldna have been easy."

Goosebumps rose along her skin as his baritone voice spoke softly near her ear. "My father and one of my uncles left to get revenge on the deaths of my youngest brother slain in battle. As soon as word reached us that they were unaccounted for, my other uncle left to join the fighting. It was a week later that all three were returned to me for burial."

Morcant's hand lightly squeezed her. "They shouldna have left you."

"I had my sister." Leana could've sworn he moved closer. She closed her eyes and fought not to lean back against him.

"Where did she go?"

Leana looked down at Morcant's hand atop hers. Her heart missed a beat when she felt his warm breath against her cheek. How was she to think coherently with him so close? Didn't he understand that he set her off-kilter, that she couldn't think of anything but his nearness? "She married a man from the village and died nine months later while birthing her first babe."

"And the bairn?"

She closed her eyes, recalling how she fought to keep the infant alive. "A fever took him. Not even my skill with herbs could save him. Just like everyone else, he left me."

CHAPTER FOUR

Morcant didn't think Leana knew how telling her words were. He could feel her pain and loneliness, the anger and resentment. His first instinct was to take her mind off of her troubles by kissing her, but something stopped him.

His body ached for relief, to sink between her thighs and seek the pleasure that awaited him. Leana's body was more than appealing. Her independence was as beautiful to him as her face and her figure.

He didn't know what stopped him from seducing her. The fact that she didn't push him away as he touched her hand and molded himself to her should have spurred him onward.

Could the darkness have changed him? Did the years there remembering Denisa and her lie alter him? Or was it the countless faces of the women he'd bedded that went through his head constantly over the two hundred years of his confinement, reminding him of the emptiness he felt in their arms that stopped him?

He wanted relief. He wanted pleasure.

But he didn't want that empty feeling in his chest that always occurred after the satisfaction wore off – and occasionally before.

Morcant found he was content to stay as he was touching Leana. He craved conversation almost as much as he longed to be touched. It hadn't hit him until that moment. His chest constricted at all he had lost – his family, his friends...his life.

How had he taken the everyday exchanges with his friends, the unintended brushes against another, or a lover's caress for granted? Morcant closed his eyes against the agony.

All of it was crashing upon him now, and he didn't think he could stand beneath the weight of it all.

When Leana's head dropped back against his chest, he brought his other hand up and set it at her waist. He wanted to turn her around and kiss her, but even the comfort they were giving each other now was enough to heave off the depression that threatened.

Morcant slowly opened his eyes. "Why have you no' found a husband?"

"So he can leave me, as well?" she asked without any heat in her words.

"You need someone to protect you."

"I protect myself. I learned how to use the bow and arrows, and I'll learn how to use the sword."

His sword. Morcant wanted it back, but he wouldn't leave her undefended to do it. As skilled as he was, he could get another weapon quickly enough. "That sword wasna made for a woman. It was meant to be in a man's large hands."

"I'll learn."

"No doubt," he whispered as he looked down at her face.

Her lashes fluttered and her eyes opened. He gazed into her sky blue eyes, lost in the utter blueness, drowning in the absolute acceptance he saw.

"You're hungry."

For much more than food, but Morcant didn't correct her. Leana had been nothing but kind. He wouldn't ruin things by seducing her only to leave her. Too many had already abandoned her. He wouldn't add his name to the list.

"I respect your independence, Leana, and even if you learn how to use the sword, against a group of men, you'll be overtaken easily."

She straightened and moved her hand from beneath his. "I know. I'm often reminded of how easily I can be overpowered."

"You're speaking of someone in particular." Morcant didn't know how he knew such a thing, only that he did. He returned to his seat, missing her touch, missing her warmth. "Who are you talking about?"

"His name is William," she said and chopped the carrot with a hard stroke. "He's been after me to marry him for years."

"So he loves you."

Leana threw him a look. "Nay. William doesn't like to be denied anything."

"If a man willna take no for an answer, it's more than just being denied."

She dumped the carrots into a pot and shrugged. "William thinks I cannot survive without a man."

"And you plan to prove him wrong?" Somehow that made Morcant smile. If there was a woman that could do it, he imagined it would be Leana.

"I've done it this long. I can continue."

Morcant never paid that much attention to women while they cooked, but he found his gaze locked on Leana. There was nothing sexual about her movements, and yet, just watching her eased the storm within him.

Had anyone told him before that he would find contentment watching a lass cook, he'd have laughed them out of his clan.

There was no doubt Leana was capable. She had to be in order to live so far from the village on her own. The spring and summer months would be the easiest for her, but the fall and winter couldn't be easy. The idea of her starving left him frowning.

"Who hunts for you?"

She pointed to the bow and quiver of arrows next to his sword. "I learned to use the bow. I also fish in the river and have my own chickens and geese. I'm not without food."

"Apparently no'," he mumbled

She used her shoulder to move hair out of her

face. "There's nothing wrong with being alone."

"Other than being lonely?" he asked. "You can no' claim no' to be lonely, lass."

Her chopping paused for a heartbeat. "On occasion."

"Do you no' want a husband and bairns?"

"I did at one time."

Intrigued, Morcant sat forward so that his arms rested on his knees. "What happened?"

"I was left alone. Then I took a good look at what was available in the village, and realized I'd rather be alone."

Morcant scratched his beard. "I doona believe a bonny lass such as yourself didna have offers from men of other clans during Highland Games and such."

"I had one or two," she said flippantly.

That's when he comprehended what she wasn't saying. "You didna want to leave your land."

"Aye." Her response was barely a whisper.

"If you were part of my clan, I wouldna allow you to remain alone. If you didna wish to marry, I'd ensure there was someone checking in on you and helping when you needed."

She chuckled, smiling over her shoulder at him. "You say that as if you've ruled a clan before."

Morcant leaned back in his chair and looked away. Until that moment, he hadn't allowed himself to think of what was now out of reach. Once again, wave after wave of regret, guilt, and fury assaulted him. All because he had let his cock rule him.

He knew that wasn't the only reason. Even if he

hadn't taken Denisa's maidenhead, he would have defended Ronan, which would likely have landed him in the same predicament.

"Morcant?"

His gaze jerked to Leana to find her half turned to him, her forehead furrowed in question. "My father was laird," he explained. "I was the second son of four. My father was killed in an ambush along with my mother, and my elder brother came close to dying. I took over while he recovered."

"And after?" she pressed.

"After, I was there for my brother. I did what was needed."

"But you enjoyed leading."

For the first time, Morcant admitted to what he hadn't even been able to confess to his friends. "Aye. Verra much."

"I know you want to find your friends, but is it wise to return to your clan?"

"Probably no', but that's the best place to begin."

She nodded and turned back to the food. "I've not stopped to ask how you're feeling. You seem to be taking all of this so...well."

"What I feel willna change how things are."

"You can't just ignore your emotions."

He smiled then. "Och, lass, but you sound like my mother."

Leana ducked her head, but he didn't miss the small smile that tilted up the corners of her mouth. She had no idea how charming she was, how uttering mesmerizing he found her.

He fisted his hands, not for his sword, but because he longed to touch her again, to slide his fingers into the long, cool length of her dark hair and hold her against him as he sampled her inviting lips.

Morcant suddenly stood. If he remained, he would do something stupid like try to touch her again. "I'm going to..." He trailed off since he didn't know what to do. "I'll be outside," he finished and stalked from the cottage.

Once outside, he drew in a deep breath and fought against the desire that raged. Would he ever be rid of it? If he eased himself now, would he find relief? He briefly thought of going to the village and finding the widow Leana had spoken of, but the thought of leaving Leana alone didn't sit right with him.

Morcant couldn't explain the silent urging telling him he had to remain close to her, as if he were being forewarned of something. He couldn't ignore the warning any more than he could pretend he wasn't adrift in a time he didn't know or belong in.

He walked to the stream and knelt against the grass before he splashed the cold water on his face. With water dripping from his beard, he looked up and let his gaze roam over the rugged landscape.

Unable to resist, he plunged his hands back into the water. How he had missed the feel of it on his hands. One of his favorite things was to swim, and he had been denied that for far too long.

There would be a loch somewhere close, and

Morcant would find it soon. Then he would spend hours in the water making up for lost time.

He dropped his chin to his chest as he pulled his hands from the stream. He was being tugged in several directions. There was his need to find out what had happened to Daman, Ronan, and Stefan, the desire to protect Leana, and then his wants like swimming, laying upon the ground and staring up at the sky, holding his sword in his hand, and riding upon a fast steed.

If he remained, he could accomplish two of the three, but then how could he face himself every day if he didn't learn about his friends?

Morcant sat, the uncomfortable weight of decisions settling over him. He hadn't minded the decisions while he acted as laird, but that was for the clan, not for himself.

As late afternoon turned into evening, Morcant watched the sun sink behind the mountains and the sky turn to orange and deep red with a smile upon his face. The sunset would be seared into his memory, not just because it was beautiful, but because it was the first time he had seen color in over two hundred years.

And he had no one to share it with. His smile faded as he thought of Leana. He wanted to call her out to join him, and as he was about to do just that, he stopped. Being too close to her was a temptation he didn't need. Leana had been kind. The least he could do was keep from touching her.

Morcant let out a breath and leaned back on his hands. As the sky darkened, it reminded him too much of his prison, causing him to become agitated and anxious. He stood and walked to the forest to gather wood. After he stacked it by the cottage, he checked the gate holding the chickens. Next, he walked the perimeter of the cottage looking for anything out of the ordinary.

Only when there was nothing else for him to do did he return to the stream and pace back and forth hoping the trickle of water would calm him as Leana did.

But it didn't.

Morcant dropped his head back as he clenched his teeth. Then he opened his eyes and saw the stars. The pinpricks of light reminded him he was no longer in the darkness.

His breathing evened and his heart stopped racing. A bright light to his left drew his gaze. Morcant turned his head and spotted the full moon that crept over the mountains. The simple beauty of it held him transfixed, captivated.

CHAPTER FIVE

Leana stood in the doorway of the cottage staring at Morcant. The way he looked at the moon hit her right in the heart. She didn't think he realized the joy and sheer delight his expression stated.

Since she had found him and he woke, he'd kept himself tightly controlled, but eventually, he would come unwound. Remorse weighed heavily upon him. Even with that weight, he stood proud and strong, almost as if daring the world to try and crush him.

She had never been courageous enough to do that. It was all she could do to face each day, and yet a small victory came with each evening.

Leana was drawn to Morcant. She couldn't deny it, nor did she want to. He placed no demands on her. He accepted her for who she was. She wondered if that was just the type of man he was, or if it was because he was in a world two centuries later than when he had last seen it?

She shook her head. Nay, Morcant might be struggling to come to terms with things, but that's not why he treated her the way he did. Perhaps that was the reason she hadn't pulled away from his touch earlier.

The simple truth was that he confused her. He made her forget her need to be independent and free of a man's rule. All Morcant made her think of was heated touches, sighs of ecstasy, and nights of pleasure.

She licked her lips, wondering what it would be like to kiss him. In all her years, she'd had only one kiss, and that had been from William when he first tried to woo her. It had been rough, sloppy, and wet.

Morcant's kiss would be the exact opposite. It was the easy way he moved, as if he were one with the world, as if he knew he owned it and didn't care what others thought that made her so certain.

His touch earlier had been light and gentle, but insistent enough so that she knew he was there. Her stomach trembled just thinking about how he had held her securely, and how she had given in and rested her head back against him.

Did he have any idea how much that little bit of weakness had cost her? She didn't think he did, nor did he fathom how much she gained from setting her burdens on his wide, thick shoulders for a short time.

Leana stepped from the cottage and made her

way toward Morcant as if some unknown force pulled them together. It frightened her, this undeniable power that ruled her body. Mostly because it felt...right.

She stopped a few feet from him. He was bathed in moonlight as he tilted his face upward with his eyes closed. The complete happiness on his face made her heart skip a beat.

"Even with my eyes closed I can see the light," he said softly. His head turned to her as his lids lifted to spear her with his topaz gaze.

That's when she realized it was the night that reminded him of his prison. She'd had a glimpse of it and knew first hand the utter darkness that once surrounded him.

Leana closed the distance between them and tugged a strand of his hair caught in his beard. "There is light all around you."

"Aye," he whispered and ran a hand down her face. His gaze intensified as he caught and held hers. "None more so than what stands before me now. You've no idea how beautiful the moonlight looks on you."

She wasn't sure how to respond. Leana began to back away, when his hand halted her with the soft grasp of her arm.

"Doona leave. Please," he pleaded. He glanced away, his smile replaced with a frown of regret. "I've been alone so long I no longer remember how to act. Forgive me if I upset you."

"It's me," she hurried to say. "I don't know how to act when receiving a compliment."

Leana could once more feel the heat of him they were so close, and again, she didn't want to move away. She wanted to be closer. All too clearly, she recalled the feel of his muscles as she had touched him earlier. Her gaze lowered to his chest. His shirt still hung open, giving her an eyeful of hard sinew.

Her mouth went dry as she thought about his shirt and kilt being gone, his body bared to her to explore as long as she wanted. The uncontrollable, irresistible need was making her forget everything else.

With her heart pounding, she raised her gaze to his face. Palpable desire hung between them. Her mouth went dry when his eyes dropped to her lips. Her lips parted of their own accord as if seeking his kiss.

"Supper is ready," she blurted out.

Just like that, a wall came down, shutting him away. "Of course."

Leana closed her eyes as he walked past. She wanted that kiss. So why had she spoken? Why couldn't she have let it happen?

Because you know he'll leave you like the others.

Yes, that was part of it, but the other part was that she was too afraid to take the chance of finding anything so wonderful, only to realize it wasn't hers to have.

Leana turned on her heel and followed Morcant into the cottage.

~ ~ ~

It was the longest night of Morcant's life. Leana's meal had been amazing, even if the conversation was stilted. She hadn't asked him to stay, and he hadn't tried to talk her into it.

She expected him to go to the village but he hadn't. Though he probably should have. Instead, Morcant remained in the woods behind Leana's cottage watching over her.

Unable to sleep, his mind was in a whirlwind. His thoughts drifted from his friends, to Ilinca who had cursed him, to the family he no longer had. However, mostly he thought of Leana.

The woman was driving him mad with desire, and she didn't even know it. He found it ironic that in the past, he would have simply moved on to another woman.

It wasn't just that he didn't want to find another woman but that no other would do. He had done no more than touch Leana, and yet the longing to have her was greater than anything he had ever experienced.

An eternity later, the sun finally broke the mountains. Morcant decided it was time to learn more about the village and the threat from the MacKay clan. Until he knew how imminent the threat was, he couldn't start to look for his friends.

~ ~ ~

Leana walked to the cottage with the hare dangling from her fingers and the bow in her other hand. It didn't take long to skin the rabbit and set it to roasting over the fire. She dusted off her hands and looked around her home. Morcant had made it seem small, but without him in it, it just seemed...empty.

Her gaze snagged on the sword. She claimed to be able to take care of herself, and in most cases she could, but Morcant was right. She couldn't stand against more than one man if attacked.

Leana grasped the pommel with her right hand, and with her left, removed the scabbard from the sword. The weapon was so heavy that she had to hold it with both hands as she walked outside.

She was never more thankful of living alone as she was when she tried to swing the sword. The weight of it caused her to lose her balance as it swung downward. She had no choice but to let go of it as she fell.

With a sigh, she climbed back to her feet and started again. Each time she fell, she got back up and kept trying. It didn't take long for her arms to begin shaking from the weight of the sword. If she continued, she was liable to take her foot off.

Leana was putting the sword back in the house when she heard a horse approach. She quickly notched an arrow and aimed it in the direction of the rider. Even when she spotted the dark red hair of William, she didn't lower the arrow. He reined his horse quickly, causing the animal to turn to the side and snort in protest.

"What are you doing, Leana?" William asked gruffly. "You know it's me."

She raised a brow. "So?"

"Lower the weapon, damn you."

"What do you want?"

He glared at her weapon a moment. "I came to see if you were all right. There's talk that someone saw you with a man yesterday."

"That's none of your concern."

"It is," he said affronted. "You're mine, Leana, you just doona realize it yet."

She rolled her eyes. "When did you hear about this strange man, William? Yesterday? Before or after you were at the pub? If you were so concerned for me, then you should've come immediately."

His face went red with anger. "That's no' fair, woman, and you know it."

"Thank you for the concern, but as I've told you, I don't need it."

"You do," he stated, his face still red as he started to dismount.

Leana pulled back the string on the bow. "I wouldn't do that unless you want this arrow in your gut. Find yourself a wife. The widow has all but thrown herself at you. Besides, you sleep in her bed nearly every night."

"How do you know that?" he demanded taken aback.

She didn't bother answering, and a heartbeat later, he swung his horse around and galloped off. Leana lowered the bow. It was a good thing William had been far enough away not to see how her arms shook holding the string.

"So that was William."

Leana jerked around to find Morcant standing at the side of the cottage with his arms crossed and a small smile playing about his wide lips. "How long have you been there?"

"Long enough to tell you that if you're going to use that sword, you're going to need someone to teach you."

She looked inside the cottage to the sword lying on the table. "It's a heavy sword."

"It was made for a man."

"You've seen swords made for women?"

He shook his head. "Nay, but that doesna mean it can no' be done."

"That's your sword."

He stared her a long while, and then gave a single nod.

"I found it just before you appeared," she explained. "Why didn't you just take it from me."

"As you said, you found it."

Leana set the bow and arrow aside. "You could've overpowered me at any time. You could've taken it when I wasn't looking."

"I'm no' that kind of man."

"Nay, you're not."

Once more, she was held by his topaz gaze. His long, sandy blonde hair was pulled back in a queue, making his face look harsher.

He dropped his arms and pushed away from the cottage. He hesitated a second before walking slowly to her. "William is a big man, but the imprint we found yesterday was bigger."

"Which means it was someone else."

"Aye. Are you worried?"

She wasn't as long as he was there, but he had to find his friends. Leana couldn't ask him to stay. It wouldn't be right. "Did you come back for your sword?"

"Nay."

"Did you come back to tell me about the boot print?"

He shook his head.

"Then why did you come back?"

"I never left."

Leana tried to hide her surprise. Her voice was breathless as she asked, "Why?"

"You, Leana. I'm here because of you."

CHAPTER SIX

"I don't understand."

Morcant wasn't sure he did either, but he wasn't going to fight the draw he had to Leana. Every time he did, it felt as if he were pushing against fate.

He halted several paces from her. "I tried leaving this morning. I got as far as the village before I turned around."

She blinked slowly, her lips parting slightly.

Morcant shrugged. "I didna even have to enter the village to discover the people are afraid. The castle near here, Ravensclyde, do you know it?"

"Aye. Everyone does," she answered.

"Apparently, the Sinclair clan has grown while I've been imprisoned. Your laird has several castles, as well as stewards. The lord of Ravensclyde is coming this way with men."

Leana rubbed her forehead as she looked around. "I see."

"War is likely coming." And for once, Morcant wasn't keen to join in.

"You think I should leave, don't you?" she asked, meeting his gaze.

"The fact your laird is sending men is good. Depending on where they set up, you might be safer here." He then moved to the wood piled at her door and chose two long sticks. Morcant tossed one to Leana. "If you're going to use a sword, then you need to know how to wield it."

"I thought you said it was too big."

"It is, but knowing how to handle a sword may one day save your life."

She swung the stick. "You would teach me?"

He liked that he surprised her. Leana thought she knew men, but she didn't know him. "First, you must keep your balance at all times. Center yourself."

Morcant demonstrated, and Leana quickly mimicked him. She was a quick study, picking up everything he taught her with ease. It wasn't long before they were sparring with the sticks. The smile on her face made something break apart in his chest, something that seemed to...free...his heart.

Every chance he got, Morcant touched her. Whether it was a brush of their bodies as he turned her one way or another, or their hands touching when he guided her arm for her. Each time he came in contact with her was like being zapped with lightning.

He easily deflected the downward arc of her stick and sidestepped to come up behind her.

Morcant grasped the long braid of her brunette locks and tugged her backward. "You should've gone left."

"Your sword was going right," she said in frustration.

Morcant turned her head by tugging on her braid so that she looked up at him. He had a hard time concentrating with her lips so close. "Watch your opponent's body, no' their eyes. My body told you I was going left while my eyes fooled you."

Silence fell between them, drowned out by the desire that raged like a wildfire. Leana's chest heaved from exertion and color infused her face. Her sky blue eyes were bright, watchful.

His gaze dropped to her mouth. Never had a woman tempted him as she did. He fought against the deluge to no avail. He hungered for a taste of her, craved to plunder her mouth until she clung to him.

The restraint he was exhibiting was something new, and he found he hated it as much as he had hated the darkness. In all his years with women, not once had he ever denied himself. He still wasn't sure why he was doing so now.

It was just a kiss. A simple kiss.

Morcant dropped his stick and wound his arm around her waist. His gaze returned to hers to discover another kind of flush had overtaken her, the flush of desire. His balls tightened in response.

His cock swelled when she also dropped her stick and turned so that she could wind her arms around his neck. If he had been uncertain of what

Leana thought of him before, he had his answer now.

Gradually, his head lowered until their lips touched. Morcant moaned at the feel of her soft mouth. He cautioned himself to go slow, but passion had him fully in its grip.

Her fingers dug into his shoulders. Morcant angled her head so that he could reach her better. He slid his tongue against her lips, seeking entry. She parted her mouth, her tongue meeting his hesitantly.

He was burning from the inside out. Leana's inexperience only heightened his desire. His hand on her braid tightened as he deepened the kiss. Pleasure erupted, engulfing them. Every time Morcant tried to slow things down, she would moan. The kiss took on a life of its own. He was mindless with need.

Somehow, he found the willpower to end the kiss. He was gasping for breath, his eyes closed as his body shook with the need to have another taste of her. Morcant rested his forehead against hers, desperate to get some measure of control.

When he cracked open his eyes, he saw Leana was as out of breath as he was. She watched him with her beautiful eyes.

"Why did you stop?" she asked in a soft whisper.

He bit back a groan. The woman had no idea how seductive she was. "Before the gypsy, I took women as I wanted. I left them pleasured, aye, but without any thought of them. I only wanted to ease myself. Two hundred years in solitude has changed me."

"Your actions, but not your desires."

Morcant shook his head. "Nay, it didna dim my desire."

He frowned as she stepped out of his arms and walked backward to the cottage. As she reached the door, she paused before she turned and walked inside.

For long moments, Morcant stayed where he was. If he went inside, he wasn't sure he could stop himself from kissing her again but neither could he walk away.

He drew in a deep breath and followed. As he stepped into the cottage, he looked around for her. Morcant finally spotted her standing by the bed with her back to him. She was unbraiding her long, dark hair.

When she finished, she shook out the length so that it fell down her back in a curtain of brunette waves that he couldn't wait to slide his fingers through. Then she turned around and locked her gaze with his. It didn't register with his brain why she had the blanket wrapped around her shoulders until she let it fall.

Whatever control he found outside vanished in an instant as he took in the sight of her nude body. Her breasts were full, but not large. Her dusky pink nipples hardened beneath his gaze, making him long to take one into his mouth.

His gaze lowered to her slim waist and gently flared hips, to the triangle of dark curls at the juncture of her thighs and down her slender legs.

"By the saints, you're beautiful."

There was no walking away now. Morcant knew it and accepted it.

He strode to her and plunged his hands into her dark locks as he dragged her against him. Her hands landed on his chest as her eyes flashed with excitement.

"Are you sure?" he asked.

Her smile was slow as it tilted upward. "More sure than I've been of anything."

Morcant hissed in a breath when her hand shoved aside his saffron shirt and met his skin. His eyes closed while she leisurely stroked his chest. His gaze snapped open when she moved. He stopped breathing when she knelt in front of him, her eyes locked with his so that her face was even with his straining cock.

Her cheek brushed against the fabric of his kilt where his arousal stood out. But it wasn't his rod that her fingers found. It was his boots. One by one she removed his boots, and then she grasped his cock through his kilt. Morcant moaned. The pleasure was exquisite, but pure torture.

Morcant unpinned his kilt and let it fall. Then he jerked off his shirt to find Leana standing before him once more.

He caressed down her arm with the backs of his fingers, completely enthralled with her. He didn't know why she had chosen him, and it didn't matter. All that concerned him was giving her pleasure.

Leana wasn't sure what had come over her. After the wild kiss that sent her reeling, she couldn't imagine not seeing where the desire would take her in Morcant's arms.

She took in the superb body before her and sighed in appreciation. Scars littered his body, proving he wasn't afraid to fight. She placed her hands on his trim waist and stroked upward to his corded stomach and thick, wide shoulders. His crisp chest hair was at odds with his warm skin. She became breathless when his arms wrapped around her, pressing her breasts against him.

Leana raised her eyes in time to see his head lower once more. As soon as their lips met, she opened her mouth for him. The fire that had taken them outside surged again. She held nothing back. Whatever he demanded, she readily gave.

The kiss grew fierce the more the passion and desire grew. His hands were everywhere, touching her, learning her. Leana was floating on a cloud of pleasure that continued to expand with each heartbeat.

Suddenly, he had her on her back on the bed. She looked up at him, watching as he bent and closed his lips around a nipple. Leana sank her fingers into the covers and moaned.

He suckled and licked first one nipple and then the other until she was moaning endlessly. Desire coiled tightly within her.

Her back arched as he skimmed his hand between her breasts down her stomach. Leana was panting, her hips moving on their own. She didn't know what would come next, but she knew as long as she was in Morcant's arms, he would take care of her.

His large hand rested on her thigh as he kissed her stomach. When he pressed her legs apart, she only hesitated a fraction of a moment.

Leana lifted her head when he settled between her legs. His gaze met hers as his mouth hovered over her sex. Then his tongue came out and he licked her.

Her head dropped back while her hips rose to meet his tongue and the pleasure that wound through her. She didn't know such bliss could be had. Leana sucked in a breath when his tongue found a spot that sent her barreling toward some unknown pinnacle.

The climax slammed into her, knocking the breath from her as wave after wave of pleasure filled her. There wasn't time for her to recover from that before he slid a finger inside her.

Leana whispered his name, as the passion grew too intense. Soon, her hips were rocking in time with his hand as his finger stretched her.

Morcant had never seen such a beautiful sight before. Leana's dark hair was spread around her, her head moving back and forth, and her soft cries of pleasure filled the cottage. Seeing her peak the first time had been amazing, but he wasn't close to being finished with her. He ached to be inside her, but he wouldn't rush anything.

He joined a second digit with the first to stretch her so she could accommodate him. As he increased his tempo, his thumb swirled around her swollen clit. That's all it took for her to orgasm again.

A satisfied smile pulled at his lips to see her body flushed with pleasure. While she was still in the throes of her climax, Morcant entered her.

She was so tight, her walls so slick that he almost spilled before he was fully inside her. He gritted his teeth and slid deeper until he felt her maidenhead. With one hard thrust, he tore through and seated himself fully.

Leana's body went taut for a moment before she relaxed. Her eyes opened to stare up at him. He smoothed her hair from her face and kissed her. As soon as she shifted her hips, he knew she was ready for more.

Morcant lifted his head and caught her gaze as began to thrust, slowly at first, but steadily building as they held each other, lost in the ecstasy.

Their bodies slid against each other as they hurtled toward pleasure. Morcant held his orgasm off as long as he could, but the moment he felt her walls clench around him, he gave in. For the first time, he found the peace that had been lacking after sharing his body with a woman.

Lost in each other's eyes, something profound and vital snapped into place within Morcant, something he knew would change him forever.

CHAPTER SEVEN

Leana fell asleep in Morcant's arms, feeling secure and sheltered as she never had before. She rested her head on his chest with his arm around her.

Sated and exhausted, Leana hovered in the place between sleep and wakefulness. She drifted through the space as if searching for something. Suddenly, she saw a man with long, dark brown hair and pale green eyes smiling down at a woman with auburn hair and gray eyes.

The vision shifted to the man riding upon a white steed with his face set in hard lines. He withdrew a sword from the scabbard at his waist as he nudged the horse into a run. Her view expanded to take in her cottage and the stream, as well as a group of men armed and ready for battle.

Leana's eyes snapped open. It took her a moment to realize she was no longer lying on

Morcant's chest. He was now leaning over her, his face lined with worry.

"You cried out. Was it a dream?" he asked.

She put her hand to her forehead and shook her head. "It was a vision."

His frown deepened. "What was it?"

"You must understand that what I see could happen tomorrow or two years from now."

"Just tell me," he urged as he took her hand and brought it to his mouth to kiss.

Leana tugged on a strip of sandy blonde hair that had come loose from his queue. "I saw a man and a woman. They were obviously in love."

"Did you recognize the couple?"

"Nay. Next, I saw the man riding upon a white horse as he drew his sword. I saw him ride into battle against the MacKays."

Morcant rolled to his back and brought her with him. "If you doona recognize the man or the woman, then what do we do?"

"Nothing. Whatever I saw is coming, which means the MacKays will attack."

"Did you notice where the battle would take place?"

Leana closed her eyes and held him tight.

"Leana?" he pressed.

"Here. The battle is here."

"Shite," Morcant stated in a low voice. "The worry I saw in the village combined with what you told me about the MacKay clan means your vision will happen soon."

She swallowed hard and opened her eyes. "I

suppose the couple could be from Ravensclyde."

"Most likely."

By his tone, Leana knew his mind was already focused on the upcoming battle. For once, she was considering going somewhere else. Perhaps she would leave with Morcant to search for Ronan and his other friends.

Leana rolled from him and rose from the bed. She walked to the table where his sword lay and lifted it in both hands. With the sword balanced between her hands, she turned back to Morcant.

"This is yours."

He slowly sat up. Then he threw off the blanket and swung his legs over the side of the bed as she approached.

She smiled at his questioning look. "You're a warrior, Morcant, a Highlander. You should never be without your sword."

"There's something else I should never be without," he said as he set aside the sword and pulled her between his legs. "You must have magic like the gypsies because you've bewitched me, Leana."

"I've no magic."

"Aye, lass, you do," he whispered.

Leana cupped his face. "You don't have to stay because of me. I know you want to search for your friends."

"I stay because I want to."

"And your friends?" she asked.

He looked away, which caused her heart to twist.

Leana licked her lips and braced herself for the inevitable. "If the gypsy put you in such a prison, it's likely she did the same to the others. Gypsies don't like to kill. They like to curse people."

"I feel as if they're still alive. Somewhere."

"Then you need to find them."

His gaze slid back to her. "You think I'm going to leave like everyone else."

It wasn't a question. "Your leaving won't be a surprise. From the beginning, I knew you wouldn't stay. I thought you left this morning."

"You think you're that easy to leave?" He posed the question in a soft voice, his gaze narrowed slightly.

Leana shrugged and let her hands drop to his shoulders. "I'm not going to trap you into staying. I don't regret making love to you. I don't regret a single moment that you've been in my life. You have an important role to play, Morcant, or the gypsy wouldn't have kept you alive."

"Important?" he asked with a snort. "No' verra, if I was taken from my family who needed me most."

"Perhaps it wasn't your family who needed you, but your friends."

"Why was I released from my prison now? Why this time? Why no' earlier or later?"

Leana shrugged as she gave a small shake of her head. "I don't know the answers."

His frown smoothed out, his face taking on a thoughtful expression. "I think I do."

"Why?"

Morcant waved away her words. "Ilinca said I would be released from the prison when I earned my freedom. I didna do anything to earn it."

"Perhaps being released was a test."

"Aye, my thoughts exactly. And if I've been released, then there is a chance that Stefan, Ronan, and Daman have, as well."

Leana felt as if Morcant were slipping further and further from her grasp. Which was silly, because she knew he was never meant to be hers to begin with.

She hadn't lied. Morcant was meant for something important, and the longer he stayed with her, the longer it would take him to find his friends and learn what it was that he was meant to do.

"You need to look for your friends. You're far from home, but they may not be," she reminded him.

He nodded absently. "Come with me."

Leana was so taken aback by his words that she could only gape at him.

"Come with me," he urged again. "What is holding you here? With a battle about to occur outside your door, why no' come with me. Help me look for my friends. Be with me."

Leana looked around the cottage. She didn't have anything holding her, but if she left, she would take a chance that Morcant would never leave her.

Was that something she could do?

Was it something she wanted to do?

"Talk to me, Leana," he urged. "What are you

thinking?"

"I don't know what to think. We just met."

He raised a brow. "I'm no' denying that, but can you honestly say you doona feel that there is something between us?"

"I don't deny it. I've not been able to ignore it since I found you lying unconscious in the woods. It's almost as if we were..." she trailed off, unable to say the words.

"Meant to be together," Morcant finished for her. "You say I'm here for a reason. I say you found me for a reason."

She wanted to accept what he said, but she knew firsthand how life could deal a terrible blow. She'd suffered through enough of them already.

"You doona want to be here for the battle," he continued. "I'll protect you as best as I can, but the middle of a war isna a place for you."

Leana ran her fingers through his hair. "Will you bring me back?"

"If that's what you want."

"It is. I ask nothing more of you."

He smiled mischievously and lightly slapped her bare bottom. "And if I want more from you?"

"We'll have to come to some sort of agreement," she said sternly, then ruined everything by laughing.

He pulled her onto the bed, and then covered her body with his. Morcant grew serious then. "You may no' realize it, but I'm no' the same man I was when I was cursed. My mother often said I was searching. I used to laugh at her, but I think she was right. None of the other women broke through my walls or caused me to feel as you do. I think I've been searching for you."

Leana blinked away the moisture that gathered in her eyes. "That's impossible. You lived two centuries before me."

"But I'm here now." He gave her a quick kiss. "Rest. We've a few hours before supper."

Morcant was thankful that she didn't argue, and even more thankful when Leana fell asleep quickly. When her breathing evened out, he rose and dressed, strapping his sword at his waist.

Then he quietly left the cottage and began to scout the area. If there was going to be a battle, that meant the MacKay clan had already chosen this area. Morcant wanted to know why. He also expected to find someone from the MacKay clan keeping watch somewhere.

The man wasn't anywhere close to Leana's, but that didn't mean he hadn't seen Morcant. If Morcant could find him, then that would give the Sinclairs a chance to stop the MacKays before an attack.

Morcant glanced back at the cottage. He hated leaving Leana alone, but it was imperative that he stop the battle before it happened. He had a terrible feeling that Leana would get caught in the middle. It left him with a knot in his chest that grew by the second.

He made his way into the woods and picked up a trail. Morcant followed it as night descended. The trail took him from one mountain to another, leading him far from Leana. Just as he was about to turn around and start again in the morning, he saw a fire in the distance. Morcant withdrew his sword and started toward it.

As he drew near, he spotted four horses and only three men sitting around the fire. Morcant knew he could take them, but he had to wait for the fourth one. He couldn't chance the man coming up behind him.

Not when he finally had something to live for.

A half hour went by with the men talking of how the upcoming battle with the Sinclairs would play out before the fourth man returned carrying a brace of hares. He tossed them down next to the three sitting before the fire. Morcant crept around to the side of the camp and plunged his sword into the one standing before they knew what was happening.

Before the other three could react, Morcant kicked one in the face and spun to dodge a blow from another sword. He yanked his sword from the first man and sunk it into the second.

He looked around for the third man and saw him disappear into the night. Morcant grimaced as he glanced down at the one he'd kicked in the face who lay with his head bleeding from hitting a rock.

Morcant doused the fire and checked to make sure the man was dead before he took off after the last foe that happened to be headed straight toward Leana's.

CHAPTER EIGHT

Leana knew it was a vision she was seeing. Perhaps it was the pounding of her heart. Maybe it was the way Morcant looked at her as if she were his entire world. Or it could be the happiness, the completeness she felt standing next to him with their hands linked.

Whatever it was, Leana felt whole for the first time since her mother had died. In the vision, she no longer felt that ever-present fear that she would always be alone.

The vision slowed, allowing her time to take it all in and really see everything. It was a first for her, and it frightened her to the marrow of her bones. But nothing like the surprise that ripped through her when she noticed the graying at Morcant's temples.

She was seeing the future – many years into the future.

Leana remained in the vision until it ended. She slowly opened her eyes, not bothering to wipe the tears that fell from the corners of her eyes and into her ears as she lay on her back.

Why had she been shown that? Why had she seen the very thing that could heal her shattered heart and give her a life she wanted more than anything?

Nothing worked like that.

Just as magic wasn't supposed to exist.

Who was she to determine what was right and what wasn't? Who was she to dare question the workings of fate or destiny?

Leana turned her head to the side, but she already knew Morcant wasn't there. She waited for the certainty that usually always came when she knew someone wasn't going to return, but she didn't feel that coldness.

She rolled off the bed and quickly washed. There was no explanation for the urgency that pushed her, but she didn't question it. Leana dressed and was in the process of brushing her hair when the ground began to shake.

There was only one thing that could cause such a tremor. Horses.

She threw open the door and stepped outside to see an army descending.

~ ~ ~

Morcant crept up the hill on his stomach, bypassing the clumps of heather and their thorns.

He reached the summit and cautiously peered over the side. His gut churned with dread when he spotted the men in the valley. They had to be from the MacKay clan. It unnerved him to realize they were so close to Leana. How had he not realized it? He should've looked farther afield when he scouted the area.

Morcant spied the man he was chasing rush toward a large, barrel-chested man with a hard face. The two exchanged words, and a moment later, the leader motioned three men to him.

It wasn't long before the three were mounted and headed out. Morcant didn't need to be there to know that the leader had sent them to Leana's. He slid out of sight and got to his feet. Morcant didn't know the area that well, but that didn't slow him as he raced toward Leana.

Morcant climbed over boulders, leapt across gaps, and used the force of running downhill to help him keep the three men in sight. The horses were faster, but they couldn't move over the terrain as he could.

His lungs burned as he pumped his legs faster. Over the next rise was Leana's cottage. She was alone, no one there to protect her. That thought made him push himself even harder.

It seemed fate was set against him. The faster he ran, the further away the men got. Still, he didn't give up. He took a chance and climbed a boulder, jumping across three of them in an effort to close the distance.

Morcant cleared the first one with no problem.

He glanced down, noting a fall would certainly break his leg. The second was just as easy until he went to jump from it to the third and his foot slipped.

He was prepared when he fell upon the third boulder on his hands and knees. His fingers helped to grip as he got his feet beneath him, and then he leapt to the ground and began running again.

As he ran up the slope, he withdrew his sword, letting out a battle cry as he did. The three men jerked their horses to a stop and faced him.

Morcant smiled when one of his opponents raced his horse toward him. The man couldn't know that was a training technique he learned from his father. Morcant continued right at the horse until the last minute where he feigned to the left, the steed missing him altogether.

The other two quickly jumped from their horses, swords at the ready, and attacked.

There was nothing so familiar as his sword in hand and a battle going on around him – even if it were three men against him. Those were usually the odds he faced, and he managed to come out the victor.

Then again, he'd had his friends to watch his back.

He was on his own this time, and it was never more apparent than when he felt a sting across his back just as he moved to the right.

Morcant pivoted and found that the third man had joined in the fight. The three attacked at once. He blocked one of the swords and punched another of the attackers in the face, and even though he tried to shift his body to dodge the oncoming sword, it still sliced across the top of his thigh.

He bellowed in fury, swinging his sword down and into the top of one of the men's shoulders. Morcant pulled his sword out of the dead man and turned to the other two as dozens more came running down the hill from Leana's.

The sound must have alerted the MacKays because in the next instant, a full-scale battle was on. Swords clang, men yelled, and blood coated everyone and everything.

Morcant bumped into someone from behind. He glanced down at the plaid and knew the man wasn't from the Sinclair or MacKay clans. They were soon fighting back to back, just as Morcant had done with his friends countless times.

~ ~ ~

Leana stood at the top of the hill, her gaze riveted on Morcant. Her stomach dropped to her feet when she saw the blood running down his right leg from a wound. There was also blood coating the back of his shirt, which meant there was an injury there, as well.

She couldn't take her eyes off the way he moved – effortlessly, gracefully...smoothly. He didn't waste a single movement. Everything he did went to cutting down his enemies as if they were nothing more than pesky insects.

"I've seen him train, but this is the first time I've truly seen him in battle."

Leana turned her head as Lady Meg came to stand beside her. Her auburn hair was in a neat braid, and her gray eyes were trained on her husband — Ronan Galt — the new lord of Ravensclyde.

Meg's eyes shifted to her. "The man you recently came across? You said his name was Morcant?"

"Aye, milady."

"Please," Meg said with a smile. "There's no need for that. What is Morcant's surname?"

Leana glanced at him again. He spun and sank his sword into an opponent that was coming at Ronan from the side. At the same moment, Ronan slashed open the chest of another who had his sword aimed at Morcant.

Ronan. It couldn't be. Could it?

Leana turned back to Meg. "It's Banner. Morcant Banner."

"I knew it," Meg said and hastily blinked her eyes. She peered at Leana hard. "What do you know of Morcant?"

If Meg's Ronan were the same Ronan that Morcant searched for, then Meg would know of the gypsies and the curse. Leana took a deep breath and said, "He appeared out of nowhere from a prison of darkness that he endured for two centuries."

Meg's hand gripped her arm. "Does Morcant remember anything?"

"Everything," Leana said. "He was getting ready to leave to search for Ronan and the others."

"They're fighting back to back and don't even know." Meg shook her head as she smiled. "I can't believe this."

Leana couldn't either. The men from Ravensclyde outnumbered the MacKay clan two to one. It didn't take the Sinclairs long to subdue their enemy.

The last two fighting were Morcant and Ronan. By the way they shifted from one side to the other fending off attacks from all sides, they had obviously done this many times. As the last of the MacKays fled back to their land, Morcant lowered his sword, his chest expanding as he took in a deep breath. Leana took a step toward him when he turned to her.

His topaz gaze met hers. She began to mentally think of all the herbs she would need for his wounds, when a smile slowly began pull up his lips. So many of Leana's family had been lost in battle that she was unaccustomed to someone like Morcant.

She smiled, the last fragments of the walls surrounding her shattering. Her heart was exposed, bare...and yet, she had never felt so shielded as she did at that moment.

Leana glanced to Morcant's left to find Ronan staring in shock. She had forgotten him for a moment, but it was time that Morcant's conscience be eased. She slid her gaze back to Morcant and tilted her head in Ronan's direction. Morcant's brow furrowed slightly, but he then turned his head and looked directly at Ronan.

"Well done," Meg said. "I think that's the first time I've seen my husband unable to find words."

Leana wanted to watch what happened between Morcant and Ronan, but her attention was called away by the men who needed their wounds tended to.

She reluctantly turned away, hoping that it wouldn't be long before Morcant returned.

~ ~ ~

It took a moment for Morcant to realize the man standing before him wasn't an illusion that his brain had created after the battle. The man's dark brown hair was still long but trimmed and neatly held back by a leather strip at the base of his neck. The pale green eyes were openly staring with a hint of doubt and bucketsful of hope.

"Morcant?"

He couldn't believe that the man standing before him was Ronan, because if it really weren't, Morcant didn't think he could handle it.

"Morcant?" Ronan said again, his head cocked a little to the side. "Is it really you? Is it really possible?"

It was the voice and the mannerisms that confirmed it for Morcant. "Ronan?"

Morcant was all smiles as Ronan pounded on his back as they embraced. He pulled back and looked into the eyes of his friend. "It really is you."

"Aye," Ronan said with a chuckle. "I didna think to ever see you again."

"I know what you mean. Where were you?"

The smile dimmed from Ronan's face. "In a place with no sound or light."

"I was in a similar place."

Ronan stepped back and looked up the hill. "I was freed by Meg."

Morcant followed his gaze to see a woman smiling down at Ronan. He immediately thought of Leana, but he couldn't find her. His first instinct was to go looking for her, then he realized she wouldn't leave her home.

"We've been married almost six months now," Ronan continued. "I never thought I could find a woman to love, much less think about marrying, and yet it happened."

"I'm happy for you." And he was, but he was also ready to be alone with Leana again, to hold her in his arms and feel her body against him.

"How were you freed?"

Morcant shrugged and turned his attention back to Ronan. "I doona know. One moment I was in the darkness, and the next I was looking up into Leana's face. I was about to set out looking for you, Daman, and Stefan."

"I've no' found anything about any of you until today." Ronan rubbed his jaw. "How long have you been out?"

"A couple of days."

"A lot can happen in a few days," Ronan said, his gaze penetrating.

Morcant merely grinned. "Aye, old friend. A verra lot can happen, like being freed from my prison, discovering a beauty who has visions of the future, learning I can no' breathe without her, and finding you again."

"It's taken me a long while to forgive Ilinca for what she did. I didna realize she did the same to you."

"I'm no' yet ready to forgive her, but I have to wonder if she knew what awaited us in the future."

Ronan shrugged and sheathed his sword. "I no longer care. If you can be here, then there's a chance that Stefan and Daman can, as well. First things first, you need to see to your wounds."

Morcant hadn't felt them until that moment. He and Ronan walked up the hill together. He still couldn't believe that it was actually Ronan beside him. But it no longer mattered how they had come to be in their dark prisons, or how they got out of them and found each other again.

Morcant reached the top of the hill and looked through the men milling about to find Leana. She moved from one man to another tending wounds. Her touch was light and her smile easy as she saw to the injuries, leaving many a man staring after her with lust in their eyes.

"She's the one who's caught your eye?" Ronan whispered.

Morcant couldn't take his eyes from her. "She's the one who captured my heart. Without even trying."

He limped away from Ronan and made his way

to Leana as she finished with her last patient. She turned and caught sight of him, halting instantly. Her long brunette tresses hung freely about her, only adding to her allure.

Without a word, she took his hand and pulled him into the cottage. He sat at the table as she knelt before him.

"You were magnificent out there," Leana said as she began to wipe the blood from him.

Morcant closed his eyes at the feel of her hands on him. "All I could think about was killing them before they reached you."

"You did it."

He sighed and opened his eyes. "With the help of Ronan. Was he who you saw in your vision on the white horse?"

"The very same," she said with a grin as she looked up from the wound on his leg. "I had no idea he was your friend. Do you know what that means, Morcant?"

"That Daman and Stefan could be out there?"

She nodded and pressed some leaves that instantly stopped the pain against the wound. "What happens now?"

"What do you mean?" There was something in her tone that worried him.

"You've found Ronan. Will you return with him to Ravensclyde?"

"No' without you."

Her blue eyes snapped to his. "You acted as laird of your clan. You know what it is to lead. You can't seriously mean not to go."

Morcant touched her face. "Ronan hasna asked it of me, but even if he does, I'm no' going anywhere without you. Why do you no' understand that? I need you, Leana, like I need the water, the sun, and the breath in my body. I don't ever want to be without you."

She stared at him, her face not showing any emotion, and Morcant knew true fear. He didn't know what he would do if she didn't want him.

"I know how much this land means to you. If you want to stay, then allow me to remain with you."

Still she didn't utter a sound.

Morcant was going to have to say the words, words he'd never thought to speak. Words he feared would scare her away. "Leana, I always thought I'd be alone. I never expected to find you. I didna even know I was looking for you." He looked down at his hands covered in blood and winced because he could only guess what he looked like after battle. "This isna the right time."

"It is," she insisted, putting her hand on his legs to keep him sitting. "Finish. Please."

Morcant frowned, unsure if she wanted to hear what he had to say, or if she just wanted him to get it over with. He parted his lips to speak when Leana held up a finger.

"Wait." She quickly and effortlessly finished cleaning his leg before winding a strip of material around it with fresh leaves. "I don't think this one needs stitching. Let me see your back."

He shifted so she could reach him. A smile

formed when she grabbed a knife and sliced off his ruined shirt. With a grunt, she set a bowl of water and a towel in front of him.

"Wipe your face and arms," she ordered as she got to work on his back.

Morcant didn't say a word as she worked and he cleaned himself. He was mystified, baffled by her, and yet he couldn't get enough.

In no time at all, she stood in front of him expectantly. Morcant blinked, anxiety taking him again now that it was time to say the words. He took her hands and got to his feet.

"You were saying you didn't know you were looking for me," she urged, her eyes bright and expectant.

The iron grip of nerves loosened their hold. "Aye, I didna know I looked for you, but I was. Now that I have found you, I doona want to let you go. Ever." Morcant swallowed hard. "I've never said these words to another woman. I love you, Leana."

Her lids closed over her eyes as she stood still. A heartbeat later, she leaned forward and rested her head on his chest as Morcant wrapped his arms around her. "I love you," she whispered.

Morcant held her tight. "It's all right, my love. I've got you, and I willna ever let you go."

"You'll need to say that every day."

"Thrice a day at the verra least," he said with a grin. He rested his chin on her head and took in a deep breath. "Is this what peace feels like?"

"I don't know. I've never felt it before. It's a

little scary."

"Aye, but we've each other."

Leana lifted her head to look into his face. "I like the sound of that."

"Then how does forever sound?"

"Amazing."

Morcant felt as if his heart would burst from his chest he was so ecstatic. He wanted to shout and dance, and at the same time he wanted to make love to Leana. A few days ago he was in Hell.

Then an angel found him and showed him heaven.

EPILOGUE

One month later...

Leana hid her grin as Morcant paced the solar of Ravensclyde as he had been doing for the past ten minutes waiting on Ronan. "You know he wouldn't leave you waiting if there weren't a reason."

"Aye," Morcant said testily. "Where the devil is he?"

"Right here," Ronan said as he entered the solar with Meg on his arm. "I apologize for the wait, my friend. I was dealing with some matters about the castle."

Leana wondered at the way Meg was grinning widely and looking between her and Morcant. Leana's gaze returned to Morcant to find his gaze narrowed on Ronan.

"Why did you call me here?" Morcant asked.

Ronan nodded a greeting at Leana. "I wanted to talk to you the day I found you, but Meg insisted the two of you needed some time alone."

"Thank you," Morcant said with a bow of his head to Meg. "Leana and I appreciate that."

Leana stood when Morcant walked to her and threaded his fingers with hers. In the month they had been together, their love had deepened. She found not only a lover, but also a friend, someone she could share her deepest desires with.

Ronan cleared his throat. "Morcant, Leana, Meg and I want to offer you both positions here as family."

Leana expected Ronan to want Morcant with him, but she hadn't expected to be included in the offer. She looked at Morcant to find him staring at her. She squeezed his hand to let him know she would support whatever decision he made.

"Morcant," Ronan said into the silence. "You know we were brothers without the bond of blood. I know you always wanted to be laird, but there's no other man I'd rather have at my back in battle."

Morcant turned to her. "What do you think?"

The fact he asked her opinion was one of the many reasons she loved him. "I want you to be happy."

"And you?"

"I'm happy wherever I am. As long as I have you."

Morcant's gaze turned dark with desire as he pulled her against him. "Ah, my bonny, Leana. To be separated by centuries, and yet we found each other – against all odds."

Leana had tears of joy filling her eyes when Morcant turned his head to Ronan and said, "We accept. Right after Leana marries me."

She laughed through her tears. "Name the place."

"Here. Now," Morcant replied with a grin. "Marry me this day, Leana."

"Aye."

Ronan's bellow for the priest was drowned out as Morcant kissed Leana completely, thoroughly, as though eternity was theirs for the taking.

Look for the next Rogues of Scotland story –
THE TEMPTED – Coming January 2015!

Until then, read on for the sneak peek at **HOT BLOODED**, the fourth book in the Dark King series…

Laith leaned back in the chair with his hands behind his head as he looked around Constantine's office. There were only a handful of Dragon Kings in the large room. Some were on various missions regarding the Dark Fae, Ulrik, and others that only Con knew about.

Still other Kings were on the sixty thousand acres of Dreagan property tending to livestock, overseeing their famous Dreagan whisky, and patrolling their borders. Because even though their dragon magic kept most humans and other beings out, some still tried to gain entrance.

As a race of shape-shifting immortals who had been around since the dawn of time, the Dragon Kings weren't without their share of enemies. And the list kept growing as the months went by.

Each King was powerful in his own right or he would never have been chosen to rule his dragons, but there was one who was King of Kings— Constantine.

Con with his surfer boy golden blond hair and soulless black eyes could be a cold son of a bitch. He did what was necessary, regardless of who was hurt, in order to keep the secret of Dreagan from leaking to the humans.

While turning the gold dragon-head cuff links at his wrist, Con sat patiently behind his desk staring at a file folder while everyone took their seats.

"What's up?" Ryder leaned over to whisper before promptly taking a bite of a jelly-filled donut.

Laith shrugged. It could be anything, and he learned long ago not to try and guess what was going on in Con's head or try to figure out Con's thinking when he did something. The fact Con wouldn't look up from the folder meant that whatever was inside was troubling indeed.

Kellan was the last to enter Con's office. After a quick look around, Kellan closed the door behind him. The Keeper of the History remained as he was, leaning against the door instead of taking a chair.

Another sign that something bad had happened. Laith took a deep breath and slowly let it out. Besides Ryder, Con, and Kellan there was Rhys, Warrick, Hal, and Tristan. Everyone looked at ease. Except for Rhys.

There was something going on with his friend, but so far Rhys hadn't shared it with anyone. The lines of strain around Rhys's mouth said that whatever bothered him was taking a hard toll.

Rhys ran a hand through his long dark hair, his gaze meeting Laith's. A heartbeat later, Rhys's gaze skated away. Laith scratched his chin, the two-day's growth of beard itching, as he considered how hard to push to get Rhys to tell him—or someone—

what was wrong.

"Come on, Con," Tristan said as he bent a leg to set his ankle atop his knee. "Stop stalling. Why did you call us in here?"

Con's black eyes slowly lifted to meet Tristan's. He let the silence lengthen before Con leaned forward and stabbed a finger on the file folder. "This."

"And what is that?" Hal's voice was calm, but as one of six Kings who had taken mates, he was anything but. His gaze was riveted on Con, his bearing anxious and worried.

Con sighed and got to his feet. He shoved his hands in the pockets of his navy slacks. "I'd hoped we would have a reprieve. I'd hoped that Kiril and Shara would have more time to themselves being newly mated."

"For the love of all that's holy, spit it out," Ryder stated, unable to wait any longer.

A muscle in Con's jaw jumped. "John Campbell was found dead this morning."

Everyone stilled, their faces expressing shock, surprise, and disbelief as Con's words penetrated. No one said a word as they comprehended what John's death meant to Dreagan.

Laith closed his eyes, feeling remorse for John's death. The Campbells had owned the fifty acres bordering Dreagan for countless generations. It began shortly after the war with the humans, once the Kings sent the dragons to another realm. There was a doorway onto Dreagan, it was hidden, but could be used by their enemies. Since no Dragon

King's magic could touch the area around the doorway, it became apparent that they would have to trust a human to do it for them.

The Campbells, one of the few groups of humans who didn't wage war on Dreagan stepped forward. And so the watch of the Campbells had begun.

Only the head of the family, the one responsible for ensuring no one accidentally stumbled upon the doorway, knew the secret of Dreagan and what it was being guarded. It continued in that vein for thousands of years through wars and invasions. The Campbells kept the Dragon Kings' secret, and the Kings, in turn, protected them.

How Laith was going to miss John's laughter and his jokes. John hadn't just protected Dreagan, he'd become a friend.

"Who's going to guard the land?" Laith asked.

Kellan glanced at Con. "John has a daughter, Iona."

"That's right. I forgot about her," Rhys said.

Hal frowned as he sat forward and rested his arms on his legs. "She's been gone for a while, aye?"

"A verra long while," Con said. "Twenty years in fact."

Laith shifted to get comfortable in the chair. "John often talked of Iona. He showed me her photographs when he'd come into the pub. For as long as I knew him, and as often as we chatted, he never told me what happened with his wife."

Con stood and walked behind his tall chair, leaning his arms upon the back. "One of John's responsibilities was to remain on the land."

"He remained when his wife left and took Iona," Hal said softly.

Laith shifted his gaze back to Con. "He could've left for that."

"He took his oath to us seriously," Kellan explained. "To help with the pain of his loss, he buried himself in his writing after that."

Warrick nodded slowly. "He was an excellent writer."

"That he was." Con looked at the file folder again.

Laith dropped his arms to his lap. "What's in the file, Con? If it was only a matter of ensuring his daughter take up her father's duties, we wouldna been called here."

"Iona stepping into her duties is another matter entirely. I'll get to that in a moment. What's in the folder is a report. John didna die by natural causes," Con said as he locked his gaze on Laith's. "He was murdered."

HOT BLOODED releases in ebook and print formats on **12.30.14**!
Get yours pre-ordered today!

Thank you for reading **The Hunger**. I hope you enjoyed it! If you liked this book – or any of my other releases – please consider rating the book at the online retailer of your choice. Your ratings and reviews help other readers find new favorites, and of course there is no better or more appreciated support for an author than word of mouth recommendations from happy readers. Thanks again for your interest in my books!

Donna Grant

www.DonnaGrant.com

ABOUT THE AUTHOR

New York Times and *USA Today* bestselling author Donna Grant has been praised for her "totally addictive" and "unique and sensual" stories. She's written more than thirty novels spanning multiple genres of romance including the bestselling Dark King stories. Her acclaimed series, Dark Warriors, feature a thrilling combination of Druids, primeval gods, and immortal Highlanders who are dark, dangerous, and irresistible. She lives with her husband, two children, a dog, and four cats in Colorado.

Connect online at:

www.DonnaGrant.com

www.facebook.com/AuthorDonnaGrant

www.twitter.com/donna_grant

www.goodreads.com/donna_grant/

Never miss a new book
From Donna Grant!

Sign up for Donna's email newsletter at
www.DonnaGrant.com

**Be the first to get notified of new releases and
be eligible for special subscribers-only exclusive
content and giveaways. Sign up today!**